For Nana

First edition 2018. Library of Congress Catalog Card Number pending. ISBN 978-0-7636-9045-8. This book was typeset in Godlike. The illustrations were done in watercolor, gouache, and ink. Candlewick Press, 99 Dover Street, Somerville, Massachusetts 02144. visit us at www.candlewick.com.
Printed in Shenzhen, Guangdong, China. 18 19 20 21 22 23 CCP 10 9 8 7 6 5 4 3 2 1

JULIÁN IS A MERMAID

Jessica Love

CANDLEWICK PRESS

This is a boy named Julián. And this is his abuela.
And those are some mermaids.

Julián LOVES mermaids.

"Vámonos, mijo. This is our stop."

"Abuela, did you see the mermaids?"

"I saw them, mijo."

"Abuela, I am also a mermaid."

"I'm going to take a bath. You be good."

Julián has a good idea.

"Oh!"

Uh-oh.

"Come here, mijo."

"For me, Abuela?"

"For you, Julián."

"Where are we going?"

"You'll see," says Abuela.

"*Mermaids,*" whispers Julián.

"Like you, mijo. Let's join them."

And they do.